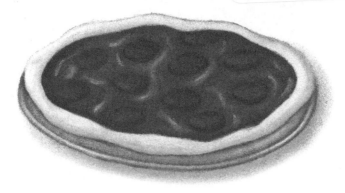

A NOTE TO PARENTS

When your children are ready to "step into reading," giving them the right books is as crucial as giving them the right food to eat. **Step into Reading Books** present exciting stories and information reinforced with lively, colorful illustrations that make learning to read fun, satisfying, and worthwhile. They are priced so that acquiring an entire library of them is affordable. And they are beginning readers with a difference—they're written on five levels.

Early Step into Reading Books are designed for brand-new readers, with large type and only one or two lines of very simple text per page. **Step 1 Books** feature the same easy-to-read type as the Early Step into Reading Books, but with more words per page. **Step 2 Books** are both longer and slightly more difficult, while **Step 3 Books** introduce readers to paragraphs and fully developed plot lines. **Step 4 Books** offer exciting nonfiction for the increasingly independent reader.

A pizza toast for a real hero:
To Felip Restrepo with love.

—r. g. g.

Text copyright © 1999 by Rita Gelman. Illustrations copyright © 1999 by Will Terry.
All rights reserved under International and Pan-American Copyright Conventions.
Published in the United States by Random House, Inc., New York, and simultaneously
in Canada by Random House of Canada Limited, Toronto.

www.randomhouse.com/kids

Library of Congress Cataloging-in-Publication Data
Gelman, Rita Golden.
Pizza Pat / by Rita Gelman ; illustrated by Will Terry. p. cm. — (Step into reading.
A step 1 book) Summary: A cumulative rhyme describes the choppy cheese, sloppy
sausages, gloppy tomatoes, and floppy dough that are cooked into a pizza and
enjoyed by dozens of mice. ISBN 0-679-89134-X (pbk.) — ISBN 0-679-99134-4
(lib. bdg.) [1. Pizza—Fiction. 2. Mice—Fiction. 3. Stories in rhyme.]
I. Terry, Will, 1956– ill. II. Title. III. Series: Step into reading. Step 1 book.
PZ8.3.G28Pi 1999 [E]—dc21 97-44609

Printed in the United States of America 10 9 8 7 6 5 4 3 2 1

STEP INTO READING and colophon are registered trademarks of Random House, Inc.

Step into Reading®

Pizza Pat

by Rita Golden Gelman
illustrated by Will Terry

A Step 1 Book

Random House 🏠 New York

This is Pat.

This is the tray
that Pat bought.

This is the dough,
all stretchy and floppy,

that lay in the tray

that Pat bought.

This is the sauce,
all gooey and gloppy,

that covered the dough,

all stretchy and floppy,

that lay in the tray

that Pat bought.

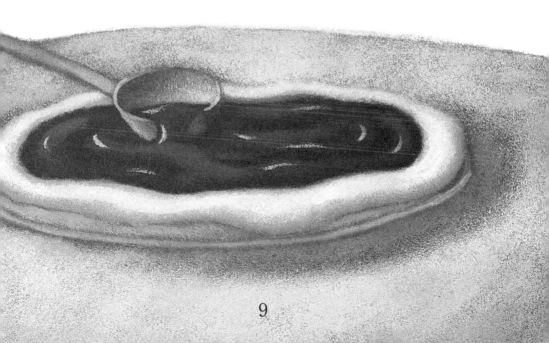

These are the sausages,
spicy and choppy,

that sat on the sauce,

all gooey and gloppy,

that covered the dough,

all stretchy and floppy,

that lay in the tray

that Pat bought.

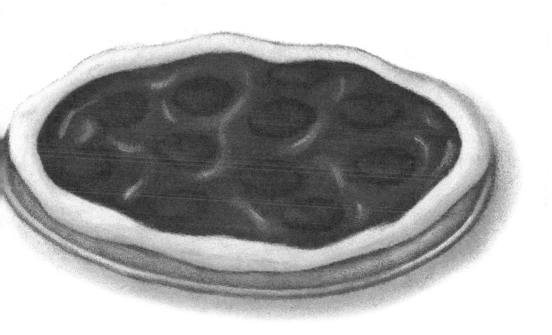

This is the cheese,
all white and sloppy,

that topped the sausages,

spicy and choppy,

that sat on the sauce,

all gooey and gloppy,

that covered the dough,

all stretchy and floppy,

that lay in the tray

that Pat bought.

This is the oven,
800 degrees,

that cooked the pizza
and melted the cheese
that topped the sausages,
spicy and choppy,
that sat on the sauce,
all gooey and gloppy,

that covered the dough,
all stretchy and floppy,
that lay in the tray
that Pat bought.

This is the pizza,
all cooked and chewy
and spicy and sloppy
and gloppy and gooey.

These are the mice,
their friends,
and their cousins.
Mice from the
neighborhood.
Mice by the dozens!

They stole the pizza,
all cooked and chewy
and spicy and sloppy
and gloppy and gooey.

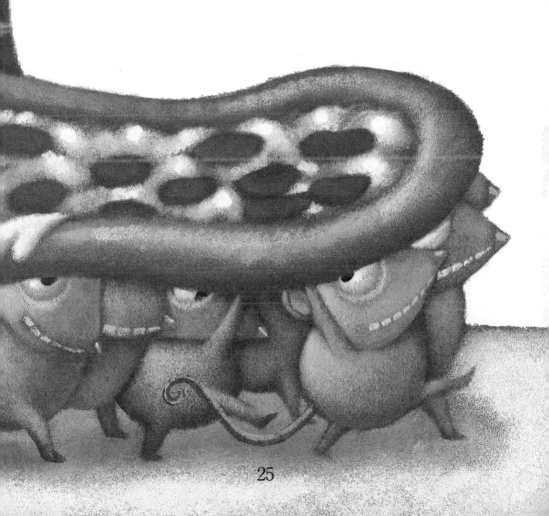

It came from the oven,
800 degrees,
that cooked the pizza
and melted the cheese
that topped the sausages,
spicy and choppy,

that sat on the sauce,

all gooey and gloppy,

that covered the dough,

all stretchy and floppy,

that lay in the tray

that Pat bought.

This is the tray
that Pat bought.

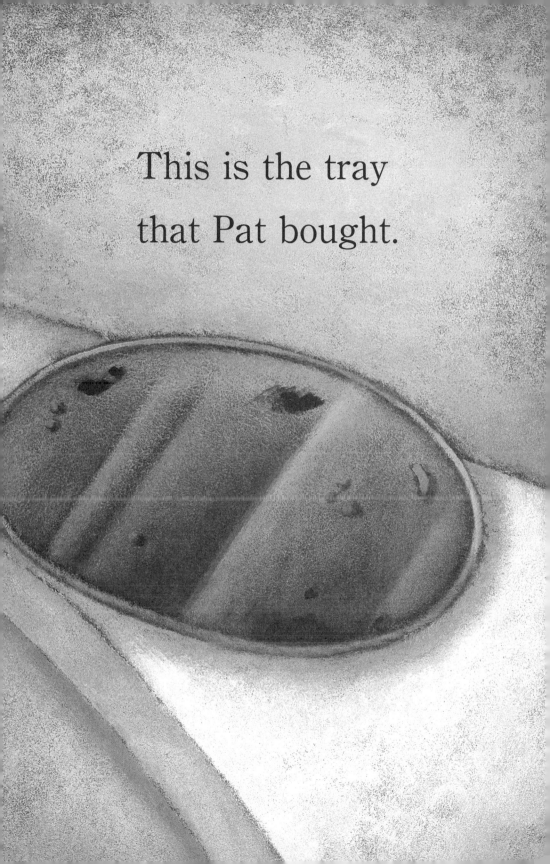

This is Pat.

Poor Pat.